CHANUKAH with ROOT & TOOTY

Written by Leah Urso   Illustrated by Yoseph Urso

© 2022 Leah & Yoseph Urso
leahurso@gmail.com
Morah Leah Publishing
www.morahleahmusic.com
ISBN: 978-1-7351941-4-1

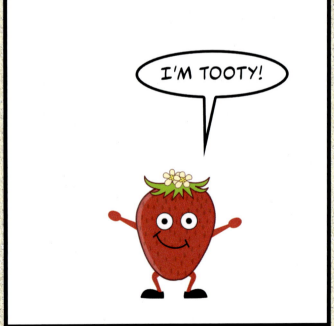

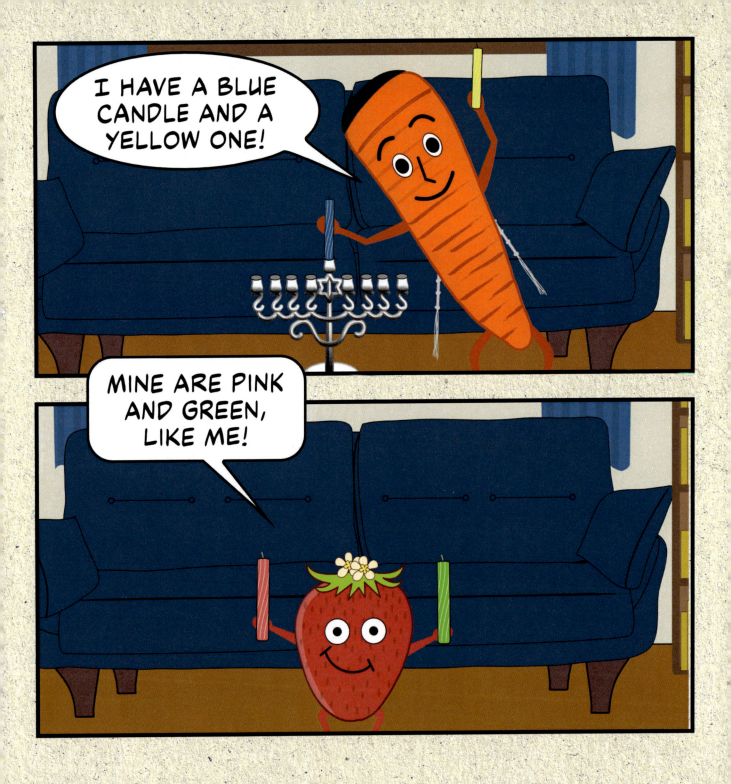

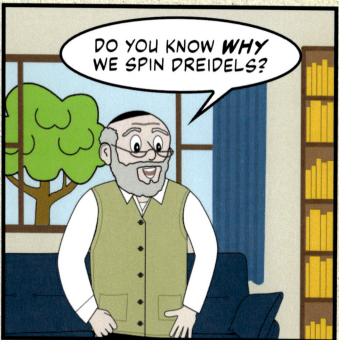

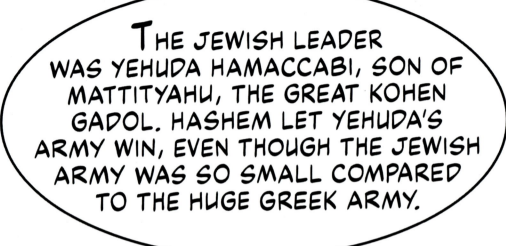

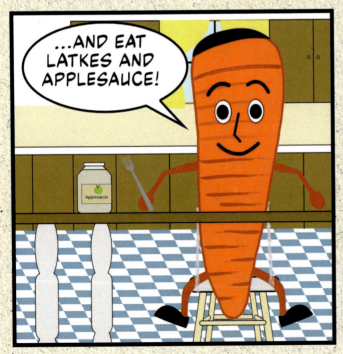

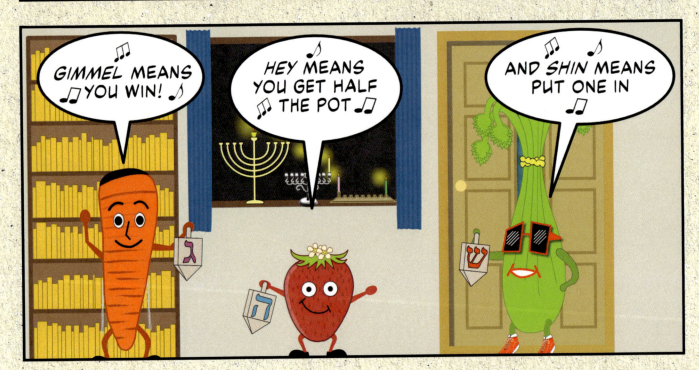

HAPPY CHANUKAH!

Made in the USA
Monee, IL
26 October 2023